Little Red Riding Hood

The Ultimate Collection

Charles Perrault, Charles Marelles, Beatrix
Potter, Clary Doty, Albert Henry Wratislaw,
Italo Calvino, Brothers Grimm

CONTENTS

LITTLE RED RIDING HOOD

LITTLE RED RIDING HOOD

BY
CHARLES PERRAULT

Once upon a time there lived in a certain village a little country girl, the prettiest creature who was ever seen. Her mother was excessively fond of her; and her grandmother doted on her still more. This good woman had a little red riding hood made for her. It suited the girl so extremely well that everybody called her Little Red Riding Hood.

One day her mother, having made some cakes, said to her, "Go, my dear, and see how your grandmother is doing, for I hear she has been very ill. Take her a cake, and this little pot of butter."

Little Red Riding Hood set out immediately to go to her grandmother, who lived in another village.

As she was going through the wood, she met with a wolf, who had a very great mind to eat her up, but he dared not, because of some woodcutters working nearby in the forest. He asked her where she was going. The poor child, who did not know that it was dangerous to stay and talk to a wolf, said to him, "I am going to see my grandmother and carry her a cake and a little pot of butter from my mother."

"Does she live far off?" said the wolf

"Oh I say," answered Little Red Riding Hood; "it is beyond that mill you see there, at the first house in the village."

"Well," said the wolf, "and I'll go and see her too. I'll go this way and go you that, and we shall see who will be there first."

The wolf ran as fast as he could, taking the shortest path, and the little girl took a roundabout way, entertaining herself by gathering nuts, running after butterflies, and gathering bouquets of little flowers. It was not long before the wolf arrived at the old woman's house. He knocked at the door: tap, tap.

"Who's there?"

"Your grandchild, Little Red Riding Hood," replied the wolf, counterfeiting her voice; "who has brought you a cake and a little pot of butter sent you by mother."

The good grandmother, who was in bed, because she was somewhat ill, cried out, "Pull the bobbin, and the latch will go up."

The wolf pulled the bobbin, and the door opened, and then he immediately fell upon the good woman and ate her up in a moment, for it been more than three days since he had eaten. He then shut the door and got into the grandmother's bed, expecting Little Red Riding Hood, who came some time afterwards and knocked at the door: tap, tap.

"Who's there?"

Little Red Riding Hood, hearing the big voice of the wolf, was at first afraid; but believing her grandmother had a cold and was hoarse, answered, "It is your grandchild Little Red Riding Hood, who has brought you a cake and a little pot of butter mother sends you."

The wolf cried out to her, softening his voice as much as he could, "Pull the bobbin, and the latch will go up."

Little Red Riding Hood pulled the bobbin, and the door opened.

The wolf, seeing her come in, said to her, hiding himself under the bedclothes, "Put the cake and the little pot of butter upon the stool, and come get into bed with me."

Little Red Riding Hood took off her clothes and got into bed. She was greatly amazed to see how her grandmother looked in her nightclothes, and said to her, "Grandmother, what big arms you have!"

"All the better to hug you with, my dear."

"Grandmother, what big legs you have!"

"All the better to run with, my child."

"Grandmother, what big ears you have!"

"All the better to hear with, my child."

"Grandmother, what big eyes you have!"

"All the better to see with, my child."

"Grandmother, what big teeth you have got!"

"All the better to eat you up with."

And, saying these words, this wicked wolf fell upon Little Red Riding Hood, and ate her all up.

Moral: Children, especially attractive, well-bred young ladies, should never talk to strangers, for if they should do so, they may well provide dinner for a wolf. I say "wolf," but there are various kinds of wolves. There are also those who are charming, quiet, polite, unassuming, complacent, and sweet, who pursue young women at home and in the streets. And unfortunately, it is these gentle wolves who are the most dangerous ones of all.

LITTLE RED CAP

BY
JACOB AND WILHELM GRIMM

Once upon a time there was a sweet little girl. Everyone who saw her liked her, but most of all her grandmother, who did not know what to give the child next. Once she gave her a little cap made of red velvet. Because it suited her so well, and she wanted to wear it all the time, she came to be known as Little Red Cap.

One day her mother said to her, "Come Little Red Cap. Here is a piece of cake and a bottle of wine. Take them to your grandmother. She is sick and weak, and they will do her well. Mind your manners and give her my greetings. Behave yourself on the way, and do not leave the path, or you might fall down and break the glass, and then there will be nothing for your sick grandmother."

Little Red Cap promised to obey her mother. The grandmother lived out in the woods, a half hour from the village. When Little Red Cap entered the woods a wolf came up to her. She did not know what a wicked animal he was, and was not afraid of him.

"Good day to you, Little Red Cap."

"Thank you, wolf."

"Where are you going so early, Little Red Cap?"

"To grandmother's."

"And what are you carrying under your apron?"

"Grandmother is sick and weak, and I am taking her some cake and wine. We baked yesterday, and they should give her strength."

"Little Red Cap, just where does your grandmother live?"

"Her house is a good quarter hour from here in the woods, under the three large oak trees. There's a hedge of hazel bushes there. You must know the place," said Little Red Cap.

The wolf thought to himself, "Now there is a tasty bite for me. Just how are you going to catch her?" Then he said, "Listen, Little Red Cap, haven't you seen the beautiful flowers that are blossoming in the woods? Why don't you go and take a look? And I don't believe you can hear how beautifully the birds are singing. You are walking along as though you were on your way to school in the village. It is very beautiful in the woods."

Little Red Cap opened her eyes and saw the sunlight breaking through the trees and how the ground was covered with beautiful flowers. She thought, "If a take a bouquet to grandmother, she will be very pleased. Anyway, it is still early, and I'll be home on time." And she ran off into the woods looking for flowers. Each time she picked one she thought that she could see an even more beautiful one a little way off, and she ran after it, going further and further into the woods. But the wolf ran straight to the grandmother's house and knocked on the door.

"Who's there?"

"Little Red Cap. I'm bringing you some cake and wine. Open the door for me."

"Just press the latch," called out the grandmother. "I'm too weak to get up."

The wolf pressed the latch, and the door opened. He stepped inside, went straight to the grandmother's bed, and ate her up. Then he took her clothes, put them on, and put her cap on his head. He got into her bed and pulled the curtains shut.

Little Red Cap had run after flowers, and did not continue on her way to grandmother's until she had gathered all that she could carry. When she arrived, she found, to her surprise, that the door was open. She walked into the parlor, and everything looked so strange that she thought, "Oh, my God, why am I so afraid? I usually like it at grandmother's." Then she went to the bed and pulled back the curtains. Grandmother was lying there with her cap pulled down over her face and looking very strange.

"Oh, grandmother, what big ears you have!"

"All the better to hear you with."

"Oh, grandmother, what big eyes you have!"

"All the better to see you with."

"Oh, grandmother, what big hands you have!"

"All the better to grab you with!"

"Oh, grandmother, what a horribly big mouth you have!"

"All the better to eat you with!" And with that he jumped out of bed, jumped on top of poor Little Red Cap, and ate her up. As soon as the wolf had finished this tasty bite, he climbed back into bed, fell asleep, and began to snore very loudly.

A huntsman was just passing by. He thought it strange that the old woman was snoring so loudly, so he decided to take a look. He stepped inside, and in the bed there lay the wolf that he had been hunting for such a long time. "He has eaten the grandmother, but perhaps she still can be saved. I won't shoot him," thought the huntsman. So he took a pair of scissors and cut open his belly.

He had cut only a few strokes when he saw the red cap shining through. He cut a little more, and the girl jumped out and cried, "Oh, I was so frightened! It was so dark inside the wolf's body!"

And then the grandmother came out alive as well. Then Little Red Cap fetched some large heavy stones. They filled the wolf's body with them, and when he woke up and tried to run away, the stones were so heavy that he fell down dead.

The three of them were happy. The huntsman took the wolf's pelt. The grandmother ate the cake and drank the wine that Little Red Cap had brought. And Little Red Cap thought to herself, "As long as I live, I will never leave the path and run off into the woods by myself if mother tells me not to."

They also tell how Little Red Cap was taking some baked things to her grandmother another time, when another wolf spoke to her and wanted her to leave the path. But Little Red Cap took care and went straight to grandmother's. She told her that she had seen the wolf, and that he had wished her a good day, but had stared at her in a wicked manner. "If we hadn't been on a public road, he would have eaten me up," she said.

"Come," said the grandmother. "Let's lock the door, so he can't get in."

Soon afterward the wolf knocked on the door and called out, "Open up, grandmother. It's Little Red Cap, and I'm bringing you some baked things."

They remained silent, and did not open the door. The wicked one walked around the house several times, and finally jumped onto the roof. He wanted to wait until Little Red Cap went home that evening, then follow her and eat her up in the darkness. But the grandmother saw what he was up to. There was a large stone trough in front of the house.

"Fetch a bucket, Little Red Cap," she said. "Yesterday I cooked some sausage. Carry the water that I boiled them with to the trough."

Little Red Cap carried water until the large, large trough was clear full. The smell of sausage arose into the wolf's nose. He sniffed and looked down, stretching his neck so long that he could no longer hold himself, and he began to slide. He slid off the roof, fell into the trough, and drowned. And Little Red Cap returned home happily and safely.

LITTLE RED HOOD

BY
ALBERT HENRY WRATISLAW

Once upon a time, there was a little darling damsel, whom everybody loved that looked upon her, but her old granny loved her best of all, and didn't know what to give the dear child for love. Once she made her a hood of red samite, and since that became her so well, and she, too, would wear nothing else on her head, people gave her the name of "Red Hood."

Once her mother said to Red Hood, "Go; here is a slice of cake and a bottle of wine; carry them to old granny. She is ill and weak, and they will refresh her. But be pretty behaved, and don't peep about in all corners when you come into her room, and don't forget to say 'Good-day.' Walk, too, prettily, and don't go out of the road, otherwise you will fall and break the bottle, and then poor granny will have nothing."

Red Hood said, "I will observe everything well that you have told me," and gave her mother her hand upon it.

But granny lived out in a forest, half an hour's walk from the village. When Red Hood went into the forest, she met a wolf. But she did not know what a wicked beast he was, and was not afraid of him.

"God help you, Red Hood!" said he.

"God bless you, wolf!" replied she.

"Whither so early, Red Hood?"

"To granny."

"What have you there under your mantle?"

"Cake and wine. We baked yesterday; old granny must have a good meal for once, and strengthen herself therewith."

"Where does your granny live, Red Hood?"

"A good quarter of an hour's walk further in the forest, under yon three large oaks. There stands her house; further beneath are the nut trees, which you will see there," said Red Hood.

The wolf thought within himself, "This nice young damsel is a rich morsel. She will taste better than the old woman; but you must

8

trick her cleverly, that you may catch both."

For a time he went by Red Hood's side Then said he, "Red Hood! Just look! There are such pretty flowers here! Why don't you look round at them all? Methinks you don't even hear how delightfully the birds are singing! You are as dull as if you were going to school, and yet it is so cheerful in the forest!"

Little Red Hood lifted up her eyes, and when she saw how the sun's rays glistened through the tops of the trees, and every place was full of flowers, she bethought herself, "If I bring with me a sweet smelling nosegay to granny, it will cheer her. It is still so early, that I shall come to her in plenty of time," and therewith she skipped into the forest and looked for flowers. And when she had plucked one, she fancied that another further off was nicer, and ran there, and went always deeper and deeper into the forest.

But the wolf went by the straight road to old granny's, and knocked at the door.

"Who's there?"

"Little Red Hood, who has brought cake and wine. Open!"

"Only press the latch," cried granny. "I am so weak that I cannot stand."

The wolf pressed the latch, walked in, and went without saying a word straight to granny's bed and ate her up. Then he took her clothes, dressed himself in them, put her cap on his head, lay down in her bed and drew the curtains.

Meanwhile little Red Hood was running after flowers, and when she had so many that she could not carry any more, she bethought her of her granny, and started on the way to her. It seemed strange to her that the door was wide open, and when she entered the room everything seemed to her so peculiar, that she thought, "Ah! My God! How strange I feel today, and yet at other times I am so glad to be with granny!"

She said, "Good-day!" but received no answer.

Thereupon she went to the bed and undrew the curtains. There lay granny, with her cap drawn down to her eyes, and looking so queer!

"Ah, granny! Why have you such long ears?"

"The better to hear you."

"Ah, granny! Why have you such large eyes?"

"The better to see you."

"Ah, granny! Why have you such large hands?"

"The better to take hold of you."

"But, granny! Why have you such a terribly large mouth?"

"The better to eat you up!"

And therewith the wolf sprang out of bed at once on poor little Red Hood, and ate her up. When the wolf had satisfied his appetite, he lay down again in the bed, and began to snore tremendously.

A huntsman came past, and bethought himself, "How can an old woman snore like that? I'll just have a look to see what it is."

He went into the room, and looked into the bed; there lay the wolf. "Have I found you now, old rascal?" said he. "I've long been looking for you."

He was just going to take aim with his gun, when he bethought himself, "Perhaps the wolf has only swallowed granny, and she may yet be released."

Therefore he did not shoot, but took a knife and began to cut open the sleeping wolf's maw. When he had made several cuts, he saw a red hood gleam, and after one or two more cuts out skipped Red Hood, and cried, "Oh, how frightened I have been; it was so dark in the wolf's maw!"

Afterwards out came old granny, still alive, but scarcely able to breathe. But Red Hood made haste and fetched large stones, with which they filled the wolf's maw, and when he woke he wanted to jump up and run away, but the stones were so heavy that he fell on the ground and beat himself to death.

Now, they were all three merry. The huntsman took off the wolf's skin; granny ate the cake and drank the wine which little Red Hood had brought, and became strong and well again; and little Red Hood thought to herself, "As long as I live, I won't go out of the road into the forest, when mother has forbidden me

LITTLE RED HAT

BY
CHRISTIAN SCHNELLER

Once there was an old woman who had a granddaughter named Little Red Hat. One day they were both in the field when the old woman said, "I am going home now. You come along later and bring me some soup."

After a while Little Red Hat set out for her grandmother's house, and she met an ogre, who said, "Hello, my dear Little Red Hat. Where are you going?"

"I am going to my grandmother's to take her some soup."

"Good," he replied, "I'll come along too. Are you going across the stones or the thorns?"

"I'm going across the stones," said the girl.

"Then I'll go across the thorns," replied the ogre.

They left. But on the way Little Red Hat came to a meadow where beautiful flowers of all colors were in bloom, and the girl picked as many as her heart desired. Meanwhile the ogre hurried on his way, and although he had to cross the thorns, he arrived at the house before Little Red Hat. He went inside, killed the grandmother, ate her up, and climbed into her bed. He also tied her intestine onto the door in place of the latch string and placed her blood, teeth, and jaws in the kitchen cupboard.

He had barely climbed into bed when Little Red Hat arrived and knocked at the door.

"Come in" called the ogre with a dampened voice.

Little Red Hat tried to open the door, but when she noticed that she was pulling on something soft, she called out, "Grandmother, this thing is so soft!"

"Just pull and keep quiet. It is your grandmother's intestine!"

"What did you say?"

"Just pull and keep quiet!"

Little Red Hat opened the door, went inside, and said, "Grandmother, I am hungry."

The ogre replied, "Go to the kitchen cupboard. There is still a little rice there."

Little Red Hat went to the cupboard and took the teeth out. "Grandmother, these things are very hard!"

"Eat and keep quiet. They are your grandmother's teeth!"

"What did you say?"

"Eat and keep quiet!"

A little while later Little Red Hat said, "Grandmother, I'm still hungry."

"Go back to the cupboard," said the ogre. "You will find two pieces of chopped meat there."

Little Red Hat went to the cupboard and took out the jaws. "Grandmother, this is very red!"

"Eat and keep quiet. They are your grandmother's jaws!"

"What did you say?"

"Eat and keep quiet!"

A little while later Little Red Hat said, "Grandmother, I'm thirsty."

"Just look in the cupboard," said the ogre. "There must be a little wine there."

Little Red Hat went to the cupboard and took out the blood. "Grandmother, this wine is very red!"

"Drink and keep quiet. It is your grandmother's blood!

"What did you say?"

"Just drink and keep quiet!"

A little while later Little Red Hat said, "Grandmother, I'm sleepy."

"Take off your clothes and get into bed with me!" replied the ogre.

Little Red Hat got into bed and noticed something hairy. "Grandmother, you are so hairy!"

"That comes with age," said the ogre.

"Grandmother, you have such long legs!"

"That comes from walking."

"Grandmother, you have such long hands!"

"That comes from working."

"Grandmother, you have such long ears!"

"That comes from listening."

"Grandmother, you have such a big mouth!"

"That comes from eating children!" said the ogre, and bam, he swallowed Little Red Hat with one gulp.

THE GRANDMOTHER

BY
ACHILLE MILLIEN

There was a woman who had made some bread. She said to her daughter, "Go and carry a hot loaf and a bottle of milk to your grandmother."

So the little girl set forth. Where two paths crossed she met the bzou [werewolf], who said to her, "Where are you going?"

"I am carrying a hot loaf and a bottle of milk to my grandmother."

"Which path are you taking? said the bzou. "The one of needles or the one of pins?"

"The one of needles," said the little girl.

"Good! I am taking the one of pins."

The little girl entertained herself by gathering needles.

The bzou arrived at the grandmother's house and killed her. He put some of her flesh in the pantry and a bottle of her blood on the shelf.

The little girl arrived and knocked at the door. "Push on the door," said the bzou. "It is blocked with a pail of water."

"Good day, grandmother. I have brought you a hot loaf and a bottle of milk."

"Put it in the pantry, my child. Take some of the meat that is there, and the bottle of wine that is on the shelf."

While she was eating, a little cat that was there said, "For shame! The slut is eating her grandmother's flesh and drinking her grandmother's blood."

"Get undressed, my child," said the bzou, and come to bed with me."

"Where should I put my apron?"

"Throw it into the fire. You won't need it anymore."

And for all her clothes -- her bodice, her dress, her petticoat, and her shoes and stockings -- she asked where she should put them, and the wolf replied, "Throw them into the fire, my child. You won't need them anymore."

When she had gone to bed the little girl said, "Oh, grandmother, how hairy you are!"

"The better to keep myself warm, my child."

"Oh, grandmother, what long nails you have!"

"The better to scratch myself with, my child!"

"Oh, grandmother, what big shoulders you have!"

"The better to carry firewood with, my child!"

"Oh, grandmother, what big ears you have!"

"The better to hear with, my child!"

"Oh, grandmother, what a big nose you have!"

"To better take my tobacco with, my child!"

"Oh, grandmother, what a big mouth you have!"

"The better to eat you with, my child!"

"Oh, grandmother, I have to do it outside!"

"Do it in the bed, my child!"

"Oh no, grandmother, I really have to do it outside."

"All right, but don't take too long."

The bzou tied a woolen thread to her foot and let her go. As soon as the little girl was outside she tied the end of the thread to a plum tree in the yard.

The bzou grew impatient and said, "Are you doing a load? Are you doing a load?"

Not hearing anyone reply, he jumped out of bed and hurried after the little girl, who had escaped. He followed her, but he arrived at her home just as she went inside.

THE TRUE HISTORY OF LITTLE GOLDEN-HOOD

BY
ANDREW LANG

You know the tale of poor Little Red Riding-Hood, that the wolf deceived and devoured, with her cake, her little butter can, and her grandmother. Well, the true story happened quite differently, as we know now. And first of all the little girl was called and is still called Little Golden-Hood; secondly, it was not she, nor the good grand-dame, but the wicked wolf who was, in the end, caught and devoured.

Only listen. The story begins something like the tale.

There was once a little peasant girl, pretty and nice as a star in its season. Her real name was Blanchette, but she was more often called Little Golden-Hood, on account of a wonderful little cloak with a hood, gold- and fire-colored, which she always had on. This little hood was given her by her grandmother, who was so old that she did not know her age; it ought to bring her good luck, for it was made of a ray of sunshine, she said. And as the good old woman was considered something of a witch, everyone thought the little hood rather bewitched too.

And so it was, as you will see.

One day the mother said to the child, "Let us see, my Little Golden-Hood, if you know now how to find your way by yourself. You shall take this good piece of cake to your grandmother for a Sunday treat tomorrow. You will ask her how she is, and come back at once, without stopping to chatter on the way with people you don't know. Do you quite understand?"

"I quite understand," replied Blanchette gaily. And off she went with the cake, quite proud of her errand.

But the grandmother lived in another village, and there was a big wood to cross before getting there. At a turn of the road under the trees, suddenly, "Who goes there?"

"Friend wolf."

He had seen the child start alone, and the villain was waiting to devour her; when at the same moment he perceived some woodcutters who might observe him, and he changed his mind. Instead of falling upon Blanchette he came frisking up to her like a good dog.

"'Tis you! my nice Little Golden-Hood," said he.

So the little girl stops to talk with the wolf, who, for all that, she did not know in the least.

"You know me, then!" said she. "What is your name?"

"My name is friend wolf. And where are you going thus, my pretty one, with your little basket on your arm?"

"I am going to my grandmother, to take her a good piece of cake for her Sunday treat tomorrow."

"And where does she live, your grandmother?"

"She lives at the other side of the wood, in the first house in the village, near the windmill, you know."

"Ah! yes! I know now," said the wolf. "Well, that's just where I'm going; I shall get there before you, no doubt, with your little bits of legs, and I'll tell her you're coming to see her; then she'll wait for you."

Thereupon the wolf cuts across the wood, and in five minutes arrives at the grandmother's house. He knocks at the door: toc, toc.

No answer.

He knocks louder.

Nobody.

Then he stands up on end, puts his two forepaws on the latch and the door opens. Not a soul in the house. The old woman had risen early to sell herbs in the town, and she had gone off in such haste that she had left her bed unmade, with her great nightcap on the pillow.

"Good!" said the wolf to himself, "I know what I'll do."

He shuts the door, pulls on the grandmother's nightcap down to his eyes, then he lies down all his length in the bed and draws the curtains.

In the meantime the good Blanchette went quietly on her way, as little girls do, amusing herself here and there by picking Easter daisies, watching the little birds making their nests, and running after the butterflies which fluttered in the sunshine.

At last she arrives at the door.

Knock, knock.

16

"Who is there?" says the wolf, softening his rough voice as best he can.

"It's me, Granny, your Little Golden-Hood. I'm bringing you a big piece of cake for your Sunday treat tomorrow."

"Press your finger on the latch, then push and the door opens."

"Why, you've got a cold, Granny," said she, coming in.

"Ahem! a little, a little . . ." replies the wolf, pretending to cough. "Shut the door well, my little lamb. Put your basket on the table, and then take off your frock and come and lie down by me. You shall rest a little."

The good child undresses, but observe this! She kept her little hood upon her head. When she saw what a figure her Granny cut in bed, the poor little thing was much surprised.

"Oh!" cries she, "how like you are to friend wolf, Grandmother!"

"That's on account of my nightcap, child," replies the wolf.

"Oh! what hairy arms you've got, Grandmother!"

"All the better to hug you, my child."

"Oh! what a big tongue you've got, Grandmother!"

"All the better for answering, child."

"Oh ! what a mouthful of great white teeth you have, Grandmother!"

"That's for crunching little children with!"

And the wolf opened his jaws wide to swallow Blanchette.

But she put down her head crying, "Mamma! Mamma!" and the wolf only caught her little hood.

Thereupon, oh dear! oh dear! he draws back, crying and shaking his jaw as if he had swallowed red-hot coals. It was the little fire-colored hood that had burnt his tongue right down his throat.

The little hood, you see, was one of those magic caps that they used to have in former times, in the stories, for making oneself invisible or invulnerable. So there was the wolf with his throat burnt, jumping off the bed and trying to find the door, howling and howling as if all the dogs in the country were at his heels.

Just at this moment the grandmother arrives, returning from the town with her long sack empty on her shoulder.

"Ah, brigand!" she cries, "wait a bit!" Quickly she opens her sack wide across the door, and the maddened wolf springs in head downwards.

It is he now that is caught, swallowed like a letter in the post. For the brave old dame shuts her sack, so; and she runs and empties it in the well, where the vagabond, still howling, tumbles in and is drowned.

"Ah, scoundrel! you thought you would crunch my little grandchild! Well, tomorrow we will make her a muff of your skin, and you yourself shall be crunched, for we will give your carcass to the dogs."

Thereupon the grandmother hastened to dress poor Blanchette, who was still trembling with fear in the bed.

"Well," she said to her, "without my little hood where would you be now, darling?" And, to restore heart and legs to the child, she made her eat a good piece of her cake, and drink a good draught of wine, after which she took her by the hand and led her back to the house.

And then, who was it who scolded her when she knew all that had happened? It was the mother.

But Blanchette promised over and over again that she would never more stop to listen to a wolf, so that at last the mother forgave her. And Blanchette, the Little Golden-Hood, kept her word. And in fine weather she may still be seen in the fields with her pretty little hood, the color of the sun. But to see her you must rise early.

THE TALE OF JEMIMA PUDDLE-DUCK

BY
BEATRIX POTTER

What a funny sight it is to see a brood of ducklings with a hen!

-- Listen to the story of Jemima Puddle-duck, who was annoyed because the farmer's wife would not let her hatch her own eggs.

Her sister-in-law, Mrs. Rebeccah Puddle-duck, was perfectly willing to leave the hatching to some one else -- "I have not the patience to sit on a nest for twenty-eight days; and no more have you, Jemima. You would let them go cold; you know you would!"

"I wish to hatch my own eggs; I will hatch them all by myself," quacked Jemima Puddle-duck.

She tried to hide her eggs; but they were always found and carried off.

Jemima Puddle-duck became quite desperate. She determined to make a nest right away from the farm.

She set off on a fine spring afternoon along the cart-road that leads over the hill.

She was wearing a shawl and a poke bonnet.

When she reached the top of the hill, she saw a wood in the distance.

She thought that it looked a safe quiet spot.

Jemima Puddle-duck was not much in the habit of flying. She ran downhill a few yards flapping her shawl, and then she jumped off into the air.

She flew beautifully when she had got a good start.

She skimmed along over the tree-tops until she saw an open place in the middle of the wood, where the trees and brushwood had been cleared.

Jemima alighted rather heavily, and began to waddle about in search of a convenient dry nesting-place. She rather fancied a tree-stump amongst some tall fox-gloves.

But -- seated upon the stump, she was startled to find an elegantly dressed gentleman reading a newspaper.

He had black prick ears and sandy coloured whiskers.

"Quack?" said Jemima Puddle-duck, with her head and her bonnet on one side -- "Quack?"

The gentleman raised his eyes above his newspaper and looked curiously at Jemima --

"Madam, have you lost your way?" said he. He had a long bushy tail which he was sitting upon, as the stump was somewhat damp.

Jemima thought him mighty civil and handsome. She explained that she had not lost her way, but that she was trying to find a convenient dry nesting-place.

"Ah! is that so? indeed!" said the gentleman with sandy whiskers, looking curiously at Jemima. He folded up the newspaper, and put it in his coat-tail pocket.

Jemima complained of the superfluous hen.

"Indeed! how interesting! I wish I could meet with that fowl. I would teach it to mind its own business!"

"But as to a nest -- there is no difficulty: I have a sackful of feathers in my wood-shed. No, my dear madam, you will be in nobody's way. You may sit there as long as you like," said the bushy long-tailed gentleman.

He led the way to a very retired, dismal-looking house amongst the fox-gloves.

It was built of faggots and turf, and there were two broken pails, one on top of another, by way of a chimney.

"This is my summer residence; you would not find my earth -- my winter house -- so convenient," said the hospitable gentleman.

There was a tumble-down shed at the back of the house, made of old soap-boxes. The gentleman opened the door, and showed Jemima in.

The shed was almost quite full of feathers -- it was almost suffocating; but it was comfortable and very soft.

Jemima Puddle-duck was rather surprised to find such a vast quantity of feathers. But it was very comfortable; and she made a nest without any trouble at all.

When she came out, the sandy whiskered gentleman was sitting on a log reading the newspaper -- at least he had it spread out, but he was looking over the top of it.

He was so polite, that he seemed almost sorry to let Jemima go home for the night. He promised to take great care of her nest until she came back again next day.

He said he loved eggs and ducklings; he should be proud to see a fine nestful in his wood-shed.

Jemima Puddle-duck came every afternoon; she laid nine eggs in the nest. They were greeny white and very large. The foxy gentleman admired them immensely. He used to turn them over and count them when Jemima was not there.

At last Jemima told him that she intended to begin to sit next day -- "and I will bring a bag of corn with me, so that I need never leave my nest until the eggs are hatched. They might catch cold," said the conscientious Jemima.

"Madam, I beg you not to trouble yourself with a bag; I will provide oats. But before you commence your tedious sitting, I intend to give you a treat. Let us have a dinner-party all to ourselves!

"May I ask you to bring up some herbs from the farm-garden to make a savoury omelette? Sage and thyme, and mint and two onions, and some parsley. I will provide lard for the stuff-lard for the omelette," said the hospitable gentleman with sandy whiskers.

Jemima Puddle-duck was a simpleton: not even the mention of sage and onions made her suspicious.

She went round the farm-garden, nibbling off snippets of all the different sorts of herbs that are used for stuffing roast duck.

And she waddled into the kitchen, and got two onions out of a basket.

The collie-dog Kep met her coming out, "What are you doing with those onions? Where do you go every afternoon by yourself, Jemima Puddle-duck?"

Jemima was rather in awe of the collie; she told him the whole story.

The collie listened, with his wise head on one side; he grinned when she described the polite gentleman with sandy whiskers.

He asked several questions about the wood, and about the exact position of the house and shed.

Then he went out, and trotted down the village. He went to look for two fox-hound puppies who were out at walk with the butcher.

Jemima Puddle-duck went up the cart-road for the last time, on a sunny afternoon. She was rather burdened with bunches of herbs and two onions in a bag.

She flew over the wood, and alighted opposite the house of the bushy long-tailed gentleman.

He was sitting on a log; he sniffed the air, and kept glancing uneasily round the wood. When Jemima alighted he quite jumped.

"Come into the house as soon as you have looked at your eggs. Give me the herbs for the omelette. Be sharp!"

He was rather abrupt. Jemima Puddle-duck had never heard him speak like that.

She felt surprised, and uncomfortable.

While she was inside she heard pattering feet round the back of the shed. Some one with a black nose sniffed at the bottom of the door, and then locked it.

Jemima became much alarmed.

A moment afterwards there were most awful noises -- barking, baying, growls and howls, squealing and groans.

And nothing more was ever seen of that foxy-whiskered gentleman.

Presently Kep opened the door of the shed, and let out Jemima Puddle-duck.

Unfortunately the puppies rushed in and gobbled up all the eggs before he could stop them.

He had a bite on his ear and both the puppies were limping.

Jemima Puddle-duck was escorted home in tears on account of those eggs.

She laid some more in June, and she was permitted to keep them herself: but only four of them hatched.

Jemima Puddle-duck said that it was because of her nerves; but she had always been a bad sitter.

RED RIDING-HOOD

BY
CLARY DOTY BATES

IF you listen, children, I will tell
The story of little Red Riding-hood:
Such wonderful, wonderful things befell
Her and her grandmother old and good
(So old she was never very well),
Who lived in a cottage in a wood.

Little Red Riding-hood, every day,
Whatever the weather, shine or storm,
To see her grandmother tripped away,
With a scarlet hood to keep her warm,
And a little mantle, soft and gay,
And a basket of goodies on her arm.

A pat of butter, and cakes of cheese,
Were stored in the napkin, nice and neat;
As she danced along beneath the trees,
As light as a shadow were her feet;
And she hummed such tunes as the bumble-bees
Hum when the clover tops are sweet.

But an ugly wolf by chance espied
The child, and marked her for his prize.
"What are you carrying there?" he cried;
"Is it some fresh-baked cakes and pies?"
And he walked along close by her side,
And sniffed and rolled his hungry eyes.

-"A basket of things for granny, it is,"
She answered brightly, without fear.
"Oh, I know her very well, sweet miss!

Two roads branch towards her cottage here;
You go that way, and I'll go this,
See which will get there first, my dear!"

He fled to the cottage, swift and sly;
Rapped softly with a dreadful grin.
"Who's there?" asked granny. "Only"
Piping his voice up high and thin.
"Pull the string and the latch will fly!"
Old granny said; and he went in.

He glared her over from foot to head;
In a second more the thing was done
He gobbled her up, and merely said,
"She wasn't a very tender one!"
And then he jumped into the bed,
And put her sack and night-cap on.

And he heard soft footsteps presently,
And then on the door a timid rap;
He knew Red Riding-hood was shy,
So he answered faintly to the tap:
Pull the string, and the latch will fly!
"She did: and granny, in her night cap,
 Lay covered almost up to her nose.
"Oh, granny dear!" she cried, "are you worse?"
"I'm all of a shiver, even to my toes!

Please won't you be my little nurse,
And snug up tight here under the clothes?"
Red Riding-hood answered, "Yes," of course.

Her innocent head on the pillow laid,
She spied great pricked-up, hairy ears,
And a fierce great mouth, wide open spread,
And green eyes, filled with wicked leers;
And all of a sudden she grew afraid;
Yet she softly asked, in spite of her fears:

"Oh, granny, what makes your ears so big?"
"To hear you with, to hear you with."
"Oh, granny, what makes your eyes so big?"
 "To see you with! to see you with!"
"Oh, granny, what makes your teeth so big?"
"To eat you with! to eat you with!"

And he sprang to Swallow her up alive;
But it chanced a woodman from the wood,
Hearing her shriek, rushed, with his knife,
And drenched the wolf in his own blood.
And in that way he saved the life
Of pretty little Red Riding-hood.

THE WOLF AND THE THREE GIRLS

BY
ITALO CALVINO

Once there were three sisters who worked in a certain town. Word reached them one day that their mother, who lived in Borgoforte, was deathly ill. The oldest sister therefore filled two baskets with four bottles of wine and four cakes and set out for Borgoforte. Along the way she met the wolf, who said to her, "Where are you going in such haste?"

"To Borgoforte to see Mamma, who is gravely ill."

"What's in those baskets?"

"Four bottles of wine and four cakes."

"Give them to me, or else—to put it bluntly—I'll eat you."

The girl gave the wolf everything and went flying back home to her sisters. Then the middle girl filled her baskets and left for Borgoforte. She too met the wolf.

"Where are you going in such haste?"

"To Borgoforte to see Mamma, who is gravely ill."

"What's in those baskets?"

"Four bottles of wine and four cakes."

"Give them to me, or else—to put it bluntly—I'll eat you."

So the second sister emptied her baskets and ran home. Then the youngest girl said, "Now it's my turn." She prepared the baskets and set out. There was the wolf.

"Where are you going in such haste?"

"To Borgoforte to see Mamma, who is gravely ill."

"What's in those baskets?"

"Four bottles of wine and four cakes."

"Give them to me, or else—to put it bluntly—I'll eat you."

The little girl took a cake and threw it to the wolf, who had his mouth open. She had made the cake especially for him and filled it with nails. The wolf caught it and bit into it, pricking his palate all over. He spat out the cake, leaped back, and ran off, shouting, "You'll pay for that! "

Taking certain short cuts known only to him, the wolf ran ahead and reached Borgoforte before the little girl. He slipped into the sick mother's house, gobbled her up, and took her place in bed.

The little girl arrived, found her mother with the sheet drawn up to her eyes, and said, "How dark you've become, Mamma!"

"That's because I've been sick so much, my child," said the wolf.

"How big your head has become, Mamma! "

"That's because I've worried so much, my child."

"Let me hug you, Mamma," said the little girl, and the wolf gobbled her up whole.

With the little girl in his belly, the wolf ran out of the house. But the townspeople, seeing him come out, chased him with pitchforks and shovels, cornered him, and killed him. They slit him open at once and out came mother and daughter still alive. The mother got well, and the little girl went back and said to her sisters, "Here I am, safe and sound!"

CATTARINETTA

BY
CHRISTIAN SCHNELLER

Once upon a time there was a mother who had a little daughter named Cattarinetta. One day she wanted to bake a cake and so she sent the girl to borrow a pan from her aunt, who was a wicked witch. The aunt gave the pan to the girl, saying, "Don't forget to bring me a piece of cake."

The cake was baked, and as soon as it was done the mother cut off a piece and put it in the pan, which the girl was to take back to the aunt. The delicious piece of cake tempted the girl, and as she walked along she pinched off one bite after the other and ate it, until finally there was nothing left in the pan. She was terrified, but she thought of a trick that would help her. She picked up a cow pie from the path and laid it in the pan so that it looked like a piece of cake with brown crust.

"Did you bring me the pan and a piece of cake?" asked the aunt as Cattarinetta arrived.

"Yes," said the girl, then set the pan down and ran away hurriedly.

Cattarinetta arrived back home, and when night fell she went to bed. Then suddenly she heard her aunt's voice calling, "Cattarinetta, I am coming. I am already at your front door!"

The girl slid further down into her bed, but the voice called out in short intervals again and again:

"Cattarinetta, I am coming. I am already on the stairway!"

"Cattarinetta, I am coming. I am already just outside your door!"

"Cattarinetta, I am coming. I am already beside your bed!"

And slurp! She swallowed up the girl.

THE WOLF-KING

BY
JOSEPH DENNIE

THE BIRDS they sung, the morning smiled,
The mother kiss'd her darling child,
And said— "My dear, take custards three,
"And carry to your grand-mummie."

The pretty maid had on her head
A little riding-hood of red,
And as she pass'd the lonely wood
They call'd her small Red-riding-hood.

Her basket on her arm she hung,
And as she went thus artless sung,
"A lady lived beneath a hill,
"Who, if not gone, resides there still."

The Wolf-King saw her pass along,
He eyed her custards, mark'd her song,
And cried— "That child and custards three,
This evening shall my supper be."

Now swift the maid pursued her way,
And heedless trill'd her plaintive lay,
Nor had she pass'd the murky wood,
When lo! the Wolf-King near her stood!

"Oh! stop, my pretty child so gay!
Oh! whither do you bend your way?"
"My little self and custards three,
Are going to my grand mummie;"

"While you by yonder mountain go,
On which the azure blue-bells grow;

I'll take this road; then haste thee, dear,
Or I before you will be there.
And when our racing shall he done,
A kiss you forfeit, if I've won;
Your prize shall be, if first you come,
Some barley-sugar and a plumb!"

"Oh! thank you, good Sir Wolf," said she,
And dropp'd a pretty courtesie;
The little maiden onward hied,
And sought the blue-belle'd mountain's side.

The Wolf sped on o'er marsh and moor,
And faintly tapp'd at granny's door;

"Oh! let me in, grand-mummy good,
For I am small Red-riding-hood."

"The bobbin pull," the grandma cried,
"The door will then fly open wide."
The crafty Wolf the bobbin drew,
And straight the door wide open flew!

He pac'd the bed-room eight times four,
And utter'd thrice an hideous roar;
He pac'd the bed-room nine times three,
And then devour'd poor grand-mummie!
He dash'd her brains out on the stones,
He gnaw'd her sinews, crack'd her bones;
He munch'd her heart, he quaff'd her gore,
And up her lights and liver tore!!!

Grand-mummy's bed he straight got in,
Her night-cap tied beneath his chin;
And waiting for his destin'd prey,
All snug between the sheets he lay.

Now at the door a voice heard he,

Which cried— "I've brought you custards three;
Oh! let me in, grand-mummy good.
For I am small red Red-riding-hood."

"The bobbin pull," the Wolf-King cried,
The door will then fly open wide!"
The little dear the bobbin drew,
And straight the door wide open flew.

She placed the custards on the floor,
And sigh'd— "I wish I'd brought you four,
I'm very tired, dear grand-mummie,
'Oh! may I come to bed to thee?"

"Oh' come." the Wolf-King softly cried,
"And lie, my sweet one, by my side;"—
Ah little thought the child so gay,
The cruel Wolf-King near her lay!

"Oh! tell me, tell me, granny dear,
"Why does your voice so gruff appear?"
"Oh' hush sweet-heart," the Wolf-King said,
"I've got a small cold in my head!"

—"Oh! tell me, grand-mummie, so kind,
Why you've a tail grows out, behind?"

Oh! hush thee, hush thee, pretty dear,
My pin-cushion I hang on there!"

"Why do your eyes so glare on me."
"They are your pretty face to see."
"Why do your ears so long appear?"
"They are your pretty voice to hear."

"Oh tell me, grammy, why, to'night,
Your teeth appear so long and white?"
Then growling, cried the Wolf so grim,
"They are to tear you limb from limb!"

His hungry teeth the Wolf-King gnash'd,
His sparkling eyes with fury flash'd,
He opened his jaws all covered with blood,
And fell on small Red-riding-hood.

He tore out bowels one and two,
"Little maid, I will eat you!"
But when he tore out three and four,
The little maid she was no more!

Take warning hence, ye children fair;
Of wolves' insidious arts beware;
And as you pass each lonely wood,
Ah! think of small Red-riding-hood.

With custards sent nor loiter slow
Nor garner blue-bells as ye go;
Get not to bed with grand-mummie,
Lest she a ravenous wolf should be!

Made in the USA
Las Vegas, NV
18 November 2020